The Escape of Alice

The Escape of Alice

A Christmas Fantasy

VINCENT STARRETT

WILDSIDE PRESS

Originally published in 1919.
Published by Wildside Press LLC.
wildsidpress.com

TO OUR FRIENDS

It has been well said, that a friend in need is a friend indeed.

Such a friend, Vincent Starrett, of Chicago, has proven to be to us.

Last year, more to our regret than to the regret of our friends, we were compelled reluctantly to forego the pleasure and privilege of holding a session with them around our fireplace or beneath our reading lamp.

And a similar situation was imminent at this Christmas time—when our good fairy, Mr. Starrett, one morning dropped on our desk *The Escape of Alice* with the cheerful message, "It is yours, Brewer, for your Christmas booklet, if you want it."

So here it is—a pleasant Christmas fantasy—sent to our friends of old and to some new ones, with all the best greetings of the season.

THE BREWERS
December 25, 1919

INTRODUCTION
by John Betancourt

V incent Starrett (October 26, 1886 – January 5, 1974) was a Canadian-born American writer, journalist, and bibliophile best known for his association with Sherlock Holmes and the world of detective fiction. Born in Toronto, Ontario, Starrett moved to Chicago early in his life, where he became a prominent figure in literary circles.

Starrett's enduring connection to Sherlock Holmes began with his book *The Private Life of Sherlock Holmes* (1933), which remains one of the most celebrated works on the legendary detective. The book is a mix of scholarship, fiction, and fan devotion, and it established Starrett as a key figure in the growing world of Sherlockian studies. His passion for Holmes also led him to become a founding member of the Baker Street Irregulars, an organization dedicated to the study and celebration of Sherlock Holmes.

In addition to his Holmes-related works, Starrett was a prolific author of mystery stories, essays, and poetry. He contributed to numerous newspapers and magazines, including *The Chicago Tribune*, where he worked as a literary columnist for several decades. His fiction often delved into the supernatural and mysterious, blending elements of horror, fantasy, and detective genres. Among his other notable works are the detective novel *The Great Hotel Murder* (1935) and the short story collection *The Quick and the Dead* (1965).

Throughout his life, Starrett was an avid collector of rare books, contributing to the world of bibliophilia with his keen literary insights and enthusiasm for mystery fiction.

THE ESCAPE OF ALICE

The red linen covers opened slightly, and a little girl slipped out, leaving behind her a curious vacancy in one of the familiar pictures signed with Mr. Tenniel's initials. She looked about her with bright, alert eyes, hoping no one had been a witness to her desertion, and then carefully began to climb down. She need not have alarmed herself, for she was no bigger than a minute, and clearer eyes than those of the rheumatic old antiquarian who kept the shop would have been needed to comprehend her departure. Fortunately, the shelf onto which she had emerged was not high, and by exercising great caution the little girl was able to reach the floor without mishap.

Still watching the old man closely, she reached a hand into the pocket of her print dress and produced a few crumbs of cake, which she immediately ate. Almost instantly she began to grow, and, in a moment, from a tiny little mite of three or four inches, she had shot up into as tall a schoolgirl of thirteen as the proudest parent could wish. The ascent, indeed, was so rapid that before she quite realized what had happened, there was her head on a level with the shelf upon which, only an instant before, she had been standing; and there was the prison from which she had escaped. "Alice's Adventures in Wonderland," read the gold letters over the door.

She plucked the volume from its place, and advanced with it toward the guardian of the bookshop.

"If it is not too high," said Alice, "I think I shall take this."

The old bookseller, whose wits had been woolgathering for many years, would not have admitted for worlds that he had not heard her enter the shop. He took the book from her hand.

"You choose wisely," he said, and patted the red covers lovingly. "Alice—the ageless child! It is one of the greatest compendiums of wit and sense in literature. There are only two books to match it. You shall have it for fifteen cents, for it is far from new, and I see what I had not noticed before, that the frontispiece is missing."

"And what are the other two?" asked Alice, eagerly.

"When you are older you will read them," said the old bookman. "They are called 'Don Quixote' and 'The Pickwick Papers'."

Then very suddenly Alice blushed, for she remembered that she could not pay. Timidly, she handed back the red-covered volume.

"I am sorry," she said, "but I have no money. I don't know why

I was so stupid as to come away without any."

"Money!" cried the antiquarian. "Did I ask you money for this book? Forgive me! It is a habit I have fallen into for which I am very sorry. Money is the least important thing in the world. Only the worthless things are to be had for money. Those things which are beyond price—thank God!—are to be had for the asking. Take it, child! Tomorrow is Christmas day. I should be grieved indeed if there were no *Alice* for you on Christmas day—as grieved as if there were no Santa Claus."

There was something so unearthly about this strange old man that Alice wondered if she were not yet in Wonderland. With a sobriety quite out of keeping with her usually merry disposition, she thanked him and went forth into the snow-clad streets.

* * * *

The plethora of Santa Clauses spending the holiday week-end in the city bewildered Alice, and now, after a long afternoon in the hurly-burly of metropolitan life, she was becoming tired. The number of Santa Clauses resident upon earth appalled her, and the extravagance of their promises, while pleasant enough, almost frightened her. Without any questions asked—even her address, which, had it been requested, would have taxed her wits rather severely—they accepted her commissions and guaranteed immediate delivery. The final excursion through the great department stores had been adventurous and diverting, but now—toward nightfall—was becoming monotonous, what with its profusion of Kris Kringles and street hawkers, and its babble of eleventh hour shoppers. It was like witnessing a really thrilling movie drama for the second time, thought Alice, who had initiated herself into the delights of moving-picture entertainment for the first time that day, and wondered at its remarkable duplication. By five o'clock the little girl knew just what each and every Santa Claus was going to say to her, and what was coming next, and that one—at least—of the three remaining Santas would want to kiss her. She had been kissed almost to death, as it was, and that was beginning to bore her, too.

It occurred to Alice, who was a shrewd little girl and not one of your bleating lambs, that Santa Claus, despite his profusion—or because of it—might be something of an old fraud, after all. She was entirely certain that not one of him resembled the jolly old saint of her mental picture. The cottony fellow at Wanacooper's was not a bit red and chubby, nor very jovial either; and she hoped that the others—at the Emporium, and the Bargain Store, and the Bon Marché—would agree more sympathetically, as to corpulence, with the merry and very dear old gentleman of her favorite poem.

She repeated the first lines, softly, under her breath:

> *'Twas the night before Christmas,*
> *And all through the house*
> *Not a creature was stirring,*
> *Not even a mouse....*

Well, that was not not surprising. Obviously, all the creatures who might otherwise have been stirring about the house on the night before Christmas were crowding and jostling each other in department stores, buying useless presents for people they didn't like. Alice thought it odd that this hadn't occurred to her before. It made the beginning of the poem quite clear.

The Santa Claus at the Emporium was entirely surrounded by children. Entirely surrounded? Why not? The schoolroom definition of an island is authority for it: "An island is a body of land entirely surrounded by water." Sticklers for accuracy will have it that the "entirely" is extraneous. If, they say, if he—or it—that is, Santa Claus or the island—is surrounded by anything (whether water or children), he—or it—is surrounded, and that is all there is to it. Not "entirely surrounded"; just surrounded. Happily, Alice knew nothing of this. As for us, we are nothing if not independent, and care nothing for grammarians—nothing at all. The Santa Claus at the Emporium was entirely surrounded by children, just like all his duplicates, and, in the midst of an alarming racket, was writing long lists of juvenile wants in a big bookkeeper's ledger. The big bookkeeper was nowhere about, and so the old fellow went right ahead, just as if it had been his own ledger, and filled as many columns as a child wished, in the most amiable manner in the world. He was the nicest Santa Claus Alice had yet seen.

He did not immediately notice Alice, who was neither larger nor smaller than most of the other children shouting around him; but when he did notice her he liked her right away. He liked the old-fashioned way of her, and her last century clothes, and from the way she looked at him he was sure that *she*, at least, believed in him, and wasn't dropping in just to see how much she could get out of him. And then he hurried, so that he could finish quickly with the others and get around to Alice. It wasn't very long until there she was—right up beside him, with his dear old whiskers tickling her shell-like ears (one of them, anyway), and his pen poised over a perfectly blank page, ready to write down anything that Alice asked him to. And his voice, too, was very pleasant.

"Now," said this kindly old saint, adjusting his eyebrows with some care, for they were slightly moth-eaten and appeared to be falling off—and no wonder, either, for some hundreds of boys and girls had been leaning against them all day—"Now," said this nice old man, "what do you wish me to bring *you* for Christmas, little Golden-hair?"

There was something charming about the way he emphasized the *you* that put Alice at ease immediately. So she told him all about the lovely doll, and the darling kitten, and the sweet bird she wanted, and had been wanting for a long time, and all about the books she needed with which to catch up on the world. For she had been locked away for so long that she felt a bit out of date, and such phrases as "League of Nations" and "Maple Nut Sundae" simply meant nothing to her, while they were the common property of every other girl and boy in the land.

The good-natured old soul wrote them all down very carefully, and then kissed Alice just as she had expected he would. He promised faithfully to deliver every one of her orders, in person, and warned her about seeing that the hearth fire was extinguished before midnight.

"Because promptly at midnight," he said, "I shall come down the chimley."

Alice giggled at that.

"You mean the chimney, don't you?" she asked.

"Chimney, indeed!" snorted Santa Claus. "After all these years, don't you think I know the difference between a chimney and a chimley? No, sir! I come down a chimley, every time. I'll leave it to everyone here."

And turning to the crowd of boys and girls around him, he asked: "How do I get into the house, children?"

"Down the chimley!" roared the chorus.

"You see?" said Santa Claus.

Alice did see, and felt very much ashamed of her display of ignorance.

"Never mind," said Santa Claus, kindly. "But I think," he added, "you had better go with my assistant, and be quite sure we have all these things in stock. He'll be glad to show you around. It's all free, you know. Just look around as long as you like, and if you see anything else you want, come right back and tell me about it."

There was a little boy standing beside Santa Claus, with a metal tag on his collar, and the generous old gentleman turned to him and told him to go and fetch his—that is, Santa Claus's—assistant. While Alice was waiting, a lot of other children pushed forward, and Alice was pretty nearly forgotten. But after a while she heard some one say, "He's coming now. He'll be here in just a minute, now," and at the same moment she saw Santa Claus's assistant coming toward her.

He was a sprightly little fellow, and Alice decided to like him. He came up in a sort of blue-green light, which danced all around him, and without the slightest hesitation Alice took his hand and walked away with him.

The little man's fingers were so cold and hard, though, that Alice was surprised, and when she was sure he wasn't looking she looked him over earnestly. After she had done that, she almost screamed, used as she was to odd things in Wonderland. For the little man was made of wood. Everything was wood, and Alice was holding on to his wooden fingers, and he was talking out of his wooden mouth, and the whole affair was the most wooden episode Alice could remember. His remarks concerning some of the books Alice wanted, the little girl thought, were the most wooden thing about him. But the little man's face was rather nice, for it was highly painted in blue and green, and he had bright yellow eyes that fairly sparkled with enamel.

"Let's see," said the wooden man. "Dolls were first on the list, weren't they? Well, here we are. We call this room 'The Kingdom of Dolls,' although as a matter of fact it is ruled by a Queen, and never did have a King, because the Queen is rather old and nobody will marry her. And as she won't allow any of the other dolls to marry until she herself finds a King, it makes it hard for the younger ones."

"Dear me," said Alice. "Do you suppose I might get a peep at the Queen, without being seen?"

"Easy enough," said the wooden man, "for there she is—that long-haired doll with the purple robe. She likes to be looked at, and I need hardly remark that her hair is false. She's awfully stuck up, though, and we won't tarry long, for she'd only snub us."

"What a funny crown she is wearing," laughed Alice, turning her head to look back.

"You may well say so," said the wooden man, ironically, "for it is made of kistletoe. She never takes it off!"

"Kistletoe!" said Alice, and then, forgetting her humiliating experience about the chimley, "Don't you mean mistletoe?"

"No, I mean kistletoe," replied the wooden man, rather impatiently. "Everybody knows what kistletoe is. But then, perhaps you are too young. When you are older you will know more."

"I'm thirteen," said Alice, with proper dignity.

"Thirteen!" shrieked the wooden man, so loudly that Alice felt sure she had offended again. "What a dreadfully unlucky number! I should be frightened to death to be thirteen. How long have you been thirteen?"

"Nearly two months now," Alice confessed, miserably. Then she brightened. "But everybody has to be thirteen sometime. Weren't you ever thirteen?"

"Never!" declared the wooden man, firmly. "When my thirteenth birthday approached, I tore off an entire year of the calendar, and passed right into my fourteenth year. Of course, there was a fearful row about it! But it's really just like skipping a grade at school. If you're smart enough you can do it. We have some very nice calendars," he added, professionally.

Alice was frankly bewildered, but she had forgotten her wounded dignity. In a moment her attention was attracted by a succession of melodious sounds, ending on a queer upward inflection that seemed to leave the phrase unfinished, and hanging in the air.

"Do listen!" she exclaimed. "Isn't that too sweet? It sounds like a bird singing."

"Most birds do," said the wooden man, drily. "That's your bird," he added, more politely. "You asked for a bird, you know."

"But why does it end its song so abruptly?" asked Alice. "It doesn't seem to finish."

"Confinement," answered the little guide, briefly. "Its cage is too small. Its notes only reach the top of the cage, and then echo back into its own ears, which naturally surprises it into silence. It's too bad, for it's losing its upper register. It once sang very well."

"I shall let it go when I get it," declared Alice, with decision.

"You may do as you please, of course," agreed the wooden man, "but you'll only be wanting another one, next Christmas."

They hurried forward, pressing through the crowd about the cage. It was humorous the way the people fell back on either side of the wooden man's sharp-elbows. What they saw, when they reached the cage, was a beautiful yellow bird with black wings, and big black eyes, swinging and singing on a perch of gold.

"Wound up too tightly," muttered the wooden man. "One of the monkeys has been monkeying with the key."

With a ferocious glare at the children around him, he reached in a hand, and Alice heard a sharp click. The bird stopped singing in the middle of a note. Then the wooden man lifted the little creature from its perch and brought it forth with as little concern as if it were made of wood, too.

"Oh!" cried Alice, in distress. "You mustn't hurt the bird! It wasn't its fault that somebody monkeyed with the key."

The word *monkeyed* puzzled her, but she supposed it was all right, since that was what the wooden man had said.

But the wooden man only laughed and held out the bird for her inspection. Then Alice saw that it was not a real bird at all, but was made of thin metal so skilfully painted as to look real.

"You forget this is Toyland," grinned the wooden man. "This bird is no more real than I am, than these children are—than you are!"

"Ain't I real?" asked Alice, in alarm. Quickly correcting herself, she said: "Am I not real?"

"Real enough," said the wooden man, casually. "A real nuisance," he muttered, under his breath; but fortunately Alice did not hear this rude remark. He continued, more pleasantly: "Oh, the bird is real enough, too. But it's been wound up too tightly. It doesn't know what it is singing, or why it is singing. It lacks a soul."

This remark was too deep for Alice, so she made no reply. After a minute, she asked:

"Aren't there any more animals?"

"Birds aren't animals," sneered the wooden man, and then he was very much ashamed of himself. "I beg your pardon," he said, contritely. "I had forgotten you are only thirteen." (He shuddered as he mentioned the sinister number.) "Well, yes, there is the Performing Pony, and the Whistling Toad, and the Talking Dog, and the Teddy Bear, and the Laughing Hyena, and the Sorrowful Snake, and the Ingenious Ibex, and the Loquacious Lynx, and—Oh, we have quite a menagerie!"

He looked quizzically at Alice, and suddenly began to sing:

> *O, ferocious and atrocious is the beast they call the*
> > *lynx;*
> *And fierce his howl, and black his scowl, and red his*
> > *jowl, methinks....*

"You have a very nice voice," said Alice, as the singer paused.

"I wish you wouldn't interrupt," snapped the wooden man. "First you want to hear about the animals, and then you don't." He stopped short. "Do you really like my voice?" he asked eagerly. Then his head drooped woodenly, for he saw that Alice was no longer paying attention.

"I haven't much of a voice myself," mused the little girl, "but I think I could speak a piece."

"Let's hear it," urged the wooden man. And moment Alice heard herself reciting:

> *I thought I heard a parson swear*
> *Because his eyes were sore;*
> *I turned around, and saw it was*
> *The watchdog's honest snore.*
> *"Alas," he whispered, tearfully,*
> *"That two times two is four!"*
>
> *I thought I saw a mastodon*
> *Upon the pantry shelf;*
> *I looked again, and saw it was*
> *A picture of myself.*
> *"O dear," I said, "the albatross*
> *Is eating all the pelf!"*

"What's pelf?" demanded the wooden man, critically.

"Pelf is—I think it's something to eat," explained Alice. "But I didn't have to say pelf, could have said elf, or delf—"

"Or skjelf!" jeered the wooden man. "Poetic license is a dangerous thing for a girl of thirteen. I shall see that yours is revoked at once."

Alice began to cry with shame and humiliation.

"There, there," cried the wooden man, ashamed of himself again. "I was only plaguing you. You rhyme beautifully—much better than I do. Now, let's go and see P. D."

"P. D.?" queried Alice, drying her tears. "Who is P. D.?"

"Why the Plausible Donkey, to be sure," laughed the wooden man. "You said you wanted to see some more animals."

"Why don't you call him D. P.?" asked Alice, after a moment, as they walked toward the menagerie.

"Why?" The wooden man seemed suspicious.

"Democratic Party," giggled Alice; and then stopped as she caught sight of the wooden man's face, which was contorted with pain. "I beg your pardon," she added, hastily.

But the wooden man wouldn't speak another word until they had arrived at the Donkey Shelter, when he became cheerful once more.

"Let me introduce you to the Plausible Donkey," he said, gallantly.

"Pleased to meet you, Mr. Donkey," said Alice, timidly. "What beautiful eyes you have."

"The better to see you with, my child," quoted the Plausible Donkey, just to show that he was not such a donkey as he looked. "What can I do for you to-day?"

"Can you sing?" asked Alice, innocently.

"Heavens!" groaned the wooden man, in her ear. "Now you've done it! He has no more voice than a crow!"

But the Plausible Donkey was pleased by the question.

"It is not surprising that you do not know my ability in that respect," he smiled, "since this is your first visit. The fact is—" He blushed modestly. "The fact is, I am descended from that notable singer, Maxwelton."

"Maxwelton!" echoed Alice, in surprise. "I thought that was a song."

"It was originally," the Plausible Donkey said plausibly. "My ancestor was named after the song because his brays were bonnie."

"Oh," said Alice, politely; but the wooden man snickered and spoiled it all.

"You're making fun of me," she cried, with tears in her voice, "and I don't want to hear you sing now."

She hurried away, leaving the wooden man to apologize as best he could for Alice's impoliteness. He was puffing mightily when he overtook her.

"I think we've had enough of animals," he said between gasps. "Let's go over and see the books." It was evident, even to Alice, that he was getting tired of his charge.

They were in the book department before they knew it—before Alice knew it, at any rate. All around them were books—heaps and heaps of them—on tables and shelves, and piled on long counters, and hung up in booths; and in the very center of the immense room, whose horizon could not be seen for the stacks of books, was a great American Eagle, made entirely of books, the work of the chief window-dresser, who was a very literary man.

"Have you 'The Young Visiters'?" asked Alice.

"Young visitors!" echoed the wooden man. "Santa Claus has dozens of them—hundreds—every day. Thousands, I guess!"

"Silly! It's a book," said Alice. "It was written by a friend of mine, Daisy Ashford, when she was only nine years old."

The wooden man looked very suspiciously at his charge.

"Nobody could write a book at nine," he said with finality.

"Daisy could, and did," declared Alice.

"Nobody could get it published, anyway," sneered the wooden man. "Of course, anybody could write one."

"And she had it published, and here it is!" cried Alice, triumphantly. She snatched a book from a long counter, and presented it to her companion.

The wooden man cautiously took it, turned it over, and handed it back.

"Where does it say she is only nine years old?" he demanded.

"In the preface, of course," answered Alice. "She's older now, but she was only nine when she wrote it."

She whirled over the leaves until she found the place.

"There it is! Sir James Barrie himself says so, in the preface."

"Humph!" said the wooden man. "He probably wrote it himself. And he wasn't nine when he wrote it, either, although he's pretty childish, at that. He's writing introductions, now, for anybody."

"He would at least know how to spell visitors, wouldn't he?"

The wooden man stared at the cover. At sight of the title he was visibly shaken.

"It might be a typographical error," he ventured. "But, if you know this Daisy Ashford, what's her book about?"

"It's about a man who—who was in love with—with a young woman," lucidly explained Alice. "He was rather an old man, and—"

"Then Barrie wrote it!" interrupted the wooden man. "That ends *that*!"

"It doesn't end anything," cried Alice, almost in tears. "And he doesn't write as many introductions as H. G. Wells, anyway!"

"O-ho!" said the wooden man. "Well?"

"Wells!" said Alice, sharply. "Wells, Wells! How many wells make a river?"

"Really," admonished the wooden man, "you mustn't get out of temper. I don't like Wells any more than you do. I find it difficult to get to the bottom of them...." He fell to singing:

Mr. Britling saw it through,
That was more than I could do!
Central, ring up Heaven's bells—
Get me God, for H. G. Wells.

Alice appeared shocked at this levity.

18

"You should not be so Leviticus," she said, "even in a good cause."

"I don't mean to be irrelevant," replied the wooden man. "I was only reviewing Mr. Wells in rhyme. Would you like to hear the next verse? It's about Amy Lowell."

"I don't believe I'd better," answered Alice, nervously. "Is she anything like Daisy Ashford?"

"They're not exactly as like as twins," admitted the wooden man. "Your Daisy is rather—er—slender, is she not?"

"Oh, very!"

"Then she's not," said the wooden man, with conviction. "I have never seen Amy Lowell, but Mr. Bitter Wynner, who was here one day last week, told me that he had got up in a street car and offered to be one of three men to give Miss Lowell a seat."

"Dear me!" exclaimed Alice. "She needs some of my cake."

"Cake?" asked the wooden man.

But Alice, fearing she had betrayed herself, would say no more about it.

"Well," said the wooden man, "we've checked on the doll, and the bird, and the books. There was to be a kitten, I believe. That means that we'll have to go back to the menagerie."

"I won't go back to the menagerie," Alice said firmly, "and if the kittens are no more polite than the donkeys, I won't have one."

"You'll have to ask Santa Claus to strike it off the list then, or you'll have it sure tomorrow morning. And we'll have to hustle, too, for the old boy closes up at eight o'clock. He went on strike for a shorter day, last month—seven hundred of him—and after eight o'clock he won't do a lick of work."

"Let's hurry," cried Alice, breathlessly.

So they hurried back through the teeming aisles, past the Plausible Donkey, who brayed after them jeeringly, past the Singing Bird, which offered to finish its song if they would only tarry, past the stuck-up Queen of the Dolls, who ogled the Wooden Man, shamefully, and at length arrived at the cottony dwelling of Santa Claus. But—alas!—the door now was closed, and tacked to the outer panel was a large sign, "Gone to the Races. Back Next Year."

"Oh!" said Alice, "isn't it provoking! Now I shall have to have a kitten, after all—and I suppose it will eat the bird, and scratch the doll, and tear up the books, and make me angry all day long."

"No doubt," said the wooden man, callously.

"But what does he mean by the races?" asked curious Alice.

"The reindeer races," replied the wooden man. "They race annually on Saturn's race track, and the winning Santa Claus is the boss Santa Claus of the year, and makes the rounds on Christmas eve. It doesn't take a minute to get there, and probably by this time the races are over."

"I hope our Santa Claus won, don't you?" cried Alice.

"What's the difference?" asked the wooden man. "They all look alike."

"That's so," said Alice, reflectively, "but this one was very nice."

"They're paid to be nice," said the wooden man cynically. "I'm paid to be nice. You don't think I've been piloting *you* round all afternoon for fun, do you?"

"Well," said Alice, with spirit, "I like that! I'm sure if I knew who paid you, I'd report you and you wouldn't get a penny. You don't deserve it, for you haven't been nice. I shall leave you, this minute."

"Good-bye," grinned the wooden man, mockingly. "Close the door after you as you go out."

* * * *

"That was a very rude wooden man," thought Alice to herself, as, half blinded with tears, she hurried through the snowy streets. "It is very evident that he tore off his thirteenth year. That is the year when people learn to be polite. And he said I was not real! I never knew till I was thirteen how real I was."

Without quite knowing where she was going, unconsciously her footsteps strayed toward the shop of the old bookman, the only friend she had found who seemed to be genuine. The precious volume, which once she had thought a prison, was safe beneath her arm. Well, she knew now what she would do. She would give it back, and if the old man were so kind as to let her, she would creep back into the pages, and be happy there again forever....

"Poor child," smiled the old bookman, when she had related her adventures, and cried over them. "Indeed he did need his thirteenth year. That is the age at which one best appreciates what reality is. Once learned, it is a lesson never to be forgotten. To the child of thirteen, all things are real if they are beautiful, and all things are unreal which are ugly. Anything is real that we want to be real. Sensible writers, like Barrie, learn this at thirteen and tear off *all* the remaining years of the calendar. Time passes, but they remain thirteen; they improve their style, their appreciation of beautiful things deepens, their outlook is broader and finer, but at heart they are still children.

They have never escaped from their thirteenth year, and they never will—and they are very glad about it."

To this astonishing harangue, Alice had no reply, for truth to tell she understood very little of it; but it sounded real, and she liked the look on the old bookman's face as he said it.

"Would you mind, sir," she timidly asked, "if I were to creep back into my book, and hide again on your shelf?"

"Are you quite sure you can manage it?" asked the old man.

"Oh, yes," said Alice, "for I still have a piece of cake that I brought with me. I had two pieces—one to make me grow, and one to make me small again. Just watch me!"

Then she took a few crumbs of cake from her pocket and began to eat them; and the old bookman standing by, saw her shrink down and down and down, until she was such a tiny little thing at his feet that his eyes could barely find her.

He picked her up gently, and opened the book lying on the counter.

"You must find the place," he said: "Do you remember it?"

With a little sigh of relief, Alice slipped into the right picture, where, to her great joy, she fitted like a glove—and suddenly the picture was complete again, and the old bookman turning the leaves over could not find her—there were so many of her, and he did not know which one was really *her*.

Suddenly the book fell from his hand, and clattered onto the floor, striking his foot as it fell. At the same instant, of course, he awoke, sitting in his chair near the old stove. He smiled a little, but was not surprised, for he was used to dreaming strange and pleasant dreams. As he stooped to pick up the book, a customer entered the store.

"What have you there?" asked the stranger, looking at the book in the old man's hand. "'Alice in Wonderland?' Charming thing! What do you ask for it?"

"Not this copy," said the old man, firmly. "This is my personal copy. This is one book you cannot buy."